THINGS MY DAD SAID

Pops Parish

ISBN Hardcover: 979-8-9922769-7-8

ISBN eBook: 979-8-9922769-6-1

First edition 2026

This book is dedicated to those mentioned within its pages, and to the many others I couldn't include in order to keep the story concise and focused. To all of you — thank you for your friendship, loyalty, and the bond you share with the Parish family.

Though this story is a work of fiction, the plot grew from my imagination and the characters — except for Suzi — were inspired by real people who have touched our lives. Some I've known for over thirty years, others for far less time, but all embody the spirit of community that continues to move me. I only hope I've done justice in capturing how truly special each of you is.

At the end of the book, you'll find a collection of idioms — phrases I've used to guide my children in understanding humanity, empathy, and loyalty. They are meant to be taken as philosophical reflections, touchstones to navigate life's complexities. Hearing them spoken among friends and family assures me there's truth in their intent. This group, especially, lives those ideals in full.

When you raise your glass, I offer these words:

To the friends we've lost and those we have found,

May our secrets stay close and our stories abound.

And when time or distance keep us apart,

Know one truth endures within each heart:

Few find the friendship we've truly sought,

For here—you are family, or you're not.

Humbly,

Pops Parish

CONTENTS

CHAPTER 1

THE CALL

Ben rolled over in bed. The morning sun peeked between the curtain and the windowsill. A bright beam of light warmed his face, welcoming him to the new day. He lay still for a few moments, resisting the urge to get up. It was a losing battle; his mind was already racing with everything he needed to accomplish today. With a sigh, Ben sat up and rubbed the sleep from his eyes.

He glanced at the other side of the bed. The sheet was thrown back, it was empty. From the sound of running water in the bathroom, he knew Suzi was in the shower. He laid back down and stared at the ceiling.

Soon, the water stopped. He heard the rustle of a towel, then footsteps returning to the bedroom. His fiancé stepped through the door, wrapped in a towel. She sat beside him on the bed. Her bobbed blonde hair was mostly dry, and her eyes sparkled as she leaned in for a quick kiss.

"Time to get up, sleepyhead," she said cheerfully.

Ben sat up and leaned back against the headboard. "I'm up. Want coffee once you're ready?"

"Sure. Oat milk and two raw sugars, please," she said, moving to the closet to pick out clothes.

Ben swung his feet to the floor and padded into the kitchen in his boxers.

"Suzi, do you want your coffee in a mug or your travel cup?" he called out.

"In my pink Rambler, please," she replied, her voice echoing softly from behind him.

Ben scooped grounds into their high-end single-serve latte machine. "Jeez," he thought, "why did I give up my ten-cup coffee pot for this contraption? It's a waste of time, energy, pretty much anything of value." But he knew why. Like much of the house, Suzi had wanted it. She'd told him on one of their earliest dates: she was high maintenance, and worth it. Ben would agree, especially in public. With friends or strangers alike, he could feel their eyes wander. He knew men, and occasionally women, looked at Suzi and envied him. Ben thought about those instances and he took some feeling of pride as he reminded himself, "She was a beautiful woman."

Suzi appeared in the kitchen fully dressed just as Ben finished vpouring oat milk into her coffee.

"Thanks, babe," she said, taking the insulated mug. "I've got to go, I've got sales to make."

"Yeah," Ben replied, trying to sound upbeat. "Early bird gets the worm."

"Eww," Suzi said, scrunching her nose. "I never liked that saying. It's kind of gross."

Ben rolled his eyes and turned back to make his own cup of coffee, black, no sugar. He briefly thought about how many times he'd watched his dad make the same exact cup when he was a kid.

"Gotta go!" Suzi called out cheerfully as she blew Ben a kiss and headed for the front door.

Ben's phone rang from the bedroom. He left the coffee machine running and went to retrieve it. Lying across the bed, he picked up the phone from the nightstand and answered.

"Hello, this is Ben."

"Ben Reese?" came a man's voice on the other end.

"Yes," Ben replied. "Who's this?"

"This is Darryl Michaud. I'm an attorney in Anchorage, Alaska."

Ben sat up on the edge of the bed. "What can I do for you, Darryl?"

There was a brief silence before Darryl said, "Mr. Reese, I hate to bring bad news. Your father has passed away, and I'm the attorney managing his estate. You're listed as the executor."

A chill swept through Ben. He hadn't spoken to his dad in, what, fourteen, fifteen years? He immediately thought of his mom, who lived on the other side of Portland, in Vancouver. His dad had been out of the picture since the divorce. Ben lingered for a second on the past, then spoke.

"Mr. Michaud, I think you might be mistaken. I can give you my mother's number if you need it. She knows that side of the family much better than I do."

Darryl was silent again. Ben couldn't tell if he was taking notes or trying to decide what to say. Finally, Ben heard, "Ben, if you didn't know, I apologize for sounding callous. I can assure you; you're the person I need to be speaking with."

Ben ran his free hand through his hair. "Okay, what is it you need?"

Darryl softened his tone. "We need to have a reading of the will. I'm sorry to have to ask you this. When can you be here to direct the final arrangements?"

Ben flushed. He had to concentrate to find the words. "Be there? In Alaska?"

Darryl's voice remained professional. "Yes. He requested to be interred in Tugat."

"What's that?" Ben asked.

"It's the town where he lived. You'll have to go there to make the final arrangements. It looks like he left everything to you."

Ben snapped to attention. "What's everything?"

Ben hadn't thought this far. Had his dad left them...him...and disappeared to become a financial success? Had his dad left him to suffer? Anger boiled low in Ben's stomach. Ben felt his jaw clench as he listened.

Darryl frowned. "It's not much, if you're thinking money. A little cash in the bank, his house, and some personal belongings." Darryl let the moment hang between them. "Ben, I knew your dad for a long time. He never had a lot, but he was a good man."

Ben struggled with the emotions that fought to surface. He steeled his resolution to get through the moment at hand. "Fine. Can you help me find a realtor? Maybe a funeral home or crematorium, if you can recommend one."

Darryl was quiet for a long moment, then spoke in a lower, more weighted tone. "Ben, this is your father we're talking about. Please... show some respect.

"Before I can close the estate," Darryl continued, "your father left some instructions that only you can carry out. While this is highly exceptional, let me read you the part of his last will and testament that you may need to understand right now. 'And it is my wish that my son, aforementioned, spread my ashes along Moose Creek near my homestead, in the presence of any and all who choose to be there. May they know that I will always be with them in good cheer and good spirit.'"

Ben sat on the edge of his bed, speechless as the words Darryl spoke soaked into his mind. Absently Ben said, "Okay, I'll be there as soon as I can. I'll let you know my flight information when I get it booked."

Darryl thanked him and hung up.

Ben's mind was a whirlwind as he got ready and left for work. The traffic on Hawthorne was always chaotic this time of morning. He drove past boutique coffee shops and vintage clothing stores that dotted the city. The squatters' tents on the sidewalks seemed fewer today. There must be a new push by the city. Were there elections recently?

Bicycles weaved through traffic like fearless cowboys herding cattle. Ben remembered when all of this used to enchant him. Today, he just wanted to get to the office and survive the day.

Ben parked in front of a building a block from his office. A giant mural covered one side of the structure. As he stepped out of the car, he took a moment to study it.

"Why would someone paint life-sized mountains when the real ones are just an hour away?" he muttered. Maybe he was just in a bad mood.

He started toward the front door, sliding his phone into his pocket, then paused to glance at the screen. The call he had received replayed in his mind. Ben hadn't seen his dad in years. His parents' divorce had been messy. His dad had an affair. His mom was devastated. The fights had been endless. Ben had been in high school. The hatred he felt for his father, for tearing their family apart, rose in him all over again.

He remembered the last time they spoke. Ben had been at a local climbing gym, the only place where he could escape the cramped apartment he shared with his mom and forget everything for a while. His dad had shown up out of the blue, talking about fresh starts and moving away. His dad had placed a hand on Ben's shoulder and asked, "Maybe you could just come check it out with me?"

Ben remembered looking at the chalk on his hands as his dad spoke, but Ben knew there was no way he'd skip graduation with his friends. He definitely wasn't going to move to the middle of nowhere with the man who had shattered what little security he'd had left.

As the awful memories resurfaced, Ben rode the elevator to his floor. When he stepped out into the hallway, he put on a big smile as he passed his coworkers. Fortunately, his cubicle was tucked in the corner, with a window overlooking the 405. Maybe watching the traffic below would help him calm down. At least he could stay busy, and no one would try to make small talk.

Ben sat at his desk, calling clients and tackling the never-ending stack of paperwork in front of him. Lunch came sooner than he expected.

Jim, who occupied a nearby cubicle, popped his head around and asked, "Hey, there's this new food truck park a couple of blocks from here. Want to check it out with me?"

Ben leaned back in his chair and tried to clear his head. "I think I'm going to eat in the lunchroom today. I've got a lot to get done."

Jim gave him a friendly slap on the shoulder, a silent I get it, before walking away. Ben watched him go, then glanced at his phone lying on the desk. The earlier conversation came back to mind.

He turned to the computer on the opposite side of his desk and typed in flights to Anchorage. He realized he didn't know how long he'd be in Alaska. Surely, he could fly up, sign the necessary documents, and return the next day. Maybe he could even pay the attorney a little extra to handle his dad's affairs in that funny-sounding town. In fact, he would fly up and—wait, what day was it? Tuesday? He could fly out Thursday and be back Friday in time to meet his friends for drinks.

Ben booked the flight and returned to work.

CHAPTER 2

INTO THE NORTH

On the drive home, he decided to call the attorney and let him know the plan. He hit the callback number, and the phone rang through the hands-free system in his car. A voicemail message blasted through the speakers: "Thank you for calling Michaud and Associates. We are unable to reach the phone currently. Please leave your message at the tone, and we will call you back during regular business hours. Beep."

"Hi, this is Ben Reese. I spoke to you this morning. I've booked my flight and will be arriving Thursday morning. I'll get your address from the website and be at your office by 10:00. If that's a problem, let me know." He ended the call. For some reason, he felt a little better.

That night, he broke the news to Suzi. She immediately said she wanted to come. He explained it would be a quick overnight trip and strictly business. He'd be home Friday and promised to make it up to her by taking her to Bacchus Bar. She finally agreed, after the appropriate amount of pouting.

Suzi had already gone when Ben woke on Thursday. He moved slowly through showering and packing for the trip. He couldn't discard the new weight he felt on his shoulders.

He loaded his car and drove mechanically to the airport. There was something soothing familiar about approaching the terminals at PDX. It seemed like the airport authorities found its way onto the news every other day. Recently the big news was the completion of the new roof. Ben walked into the main lobby and looked skyward at the inverted wicker basket maze of wood and metal that adorned the ceiling. He did have to admit it was pretty impressive. Portland definitely had its own style. It was one reason Ben enjoyed living there.

The flight took almost four hours. It felt like minutes as Ben fell back on an old habit of going to sleep as soon as he was seated on the plane. He woke with his head pressed firmly against the cabin wall.

He gathered his carry-on bag and exited as quickly as he could. He stepped from the plane into the airport's waiting area. The airport was relatively small. The first thing he noticed was a twelve-foot stuffed polar bear standing in a frozen attack pose at the far end of the room. It startled him. He'd seen bears in zoos before, but this one was a monster.

Ben slung his carry-on backpack over his shoulder and headed to the loading and unloading area outside. Traffic was light, and two cabs waited at one end. "Do people even use cabs anymore?" he wondered to himself, "Evidently that's still an option here in the untamed North." He approached the closer one and got into the back seat. The driver, an older, heavyset man who looked more like a Vietnam vet than a cabbie, asked for the address.

"Downtown, please," Ben responded as he made himself comfortable.

The cab driver quietly sat with his hands on the steering wheel. He locked eyes with Ben in the rear-view mirror. Ben furrowed his brow in silent protest. The driver sighed and asked, "Anywhere specific downtown?"

"I have a meeting," Ben started as he opened his phone and began searching for the office address he had saved after his conversation with Darryl. "Six hundred block of West Sixth Street."

The cab driver nodded his head self-assuredly and put the cab into gear. He turned up the radio volume as it announced, "Alaska rocks to K-WHALE." The cool summer breeze whipped through the driver's open window and Ben's stomach sank in anticipation of talking to Darryl.

The block was dominated by one large office building, which was the least colorful thing Ben had seen so far in this trip. Gray and square, the building looked like something left by the Soviets. Inside, he scanned the business directory posted in the wide hallway on the first floor and took the elevator up to the attorney's office. Darryl met him at the door. Ben felt immediately more comfortable around Darryl. It wasn't his short black hair that seemed to be fighting a losing battle against suddenly becoming unkempt or the ever present feeling he gave that he was about to burst into laughter at some private joke you didn't know. Maybe it was his dark eyes that stripped away any pretense of potential for untruth as he raptly paid attention to every word you said. While Ben was sure that Darryl unnerved some people, Ben felt an instant bond.

"Come in," Darryl said. "My secretary's out at the moment. If you want coffee or something…"

Ben shook his head politely. "I'd really like to get this done. I haven't been to the hotel yet."

"Well," Darryl said, "come sit down in my office. I've got the Last Will and Testament on my desk."

Ben walked into the small office and sat across from Darryl. The window behind Darryl framed the forest and mountains surrounding the city, it was picturesque, almost magnetic.

His gaze wandered around the room. There was a small shelf with a Moose

Run 10k trophy, a couple of ribbons and a framed picture of Darryl wearing a t-shirt that boldly said My Sport Is Your Punishment.

Near the shelf was a small framed picture hanging on the wall. It wasn't of people or a landscape. Inside the frame were printed words: "#8: Only moderation in excess." The oxymoron wasn't wasted on Ben and made him smile.

After Ben signed the relevant documents, Darryl slid an urn adorned with a salmon and starry night sky across the desk to him. Ben took the cool ceramic in his hands and studied the art. Tiny lines of paint raised the scene under the touch of his fingers as he traced them. He could feel a weight that could not be expressed physically that he shared with the object in his hands.

He found a hotel within walking distance of the office building.

The next morning, Ben woke. He hadn't slept well and was still exhausted. He lingered on the idea that this trip was going to take longer than he expected. He would need to let Suzi know and that wasn't a conversation he wanted to have. She would be upset and he didn't want the burden of guilt of letting her down. After getting ready for the day, he ate breakfast in the hotel lobby. By the time he'd

Ubered back to the airport and rented a car, it was already mid-morning. Ben typed "Blue Sky Tavern" into the GPS and started driving.

Living in Oregon, Ben was no stranger to beautiful scenery, but Alaska felt different. Mounts Hood and Saint Helen could be seen on a clear day, but the mountains surrounding Anchorage on three sides were ever-present, and as he drove north, they stretched along the highway like silent guides leading him forward. He could even see patches of snow near the top of a few. The air felt cleaner, and everything seemed… bigger.

It didn't take long to leave the city behind. The commercial buildings gave way to tall, green forests sprinkled with the occasional house or crystal-blue stream that seemed to erupt randomly from the earth. Cars and people became fewer and fewer. An hour from town, Ben was driving through thick pines that blocked most of the view except straight above him.

When he finally broke free of the forest, Mount McKinley rose in the distance and commanded his attention. The tallest peak in North America stood majestic and snow-capped in the middle of summer, set beneath a shade of blue sky he'd never seen before. A powerful river rushed along the right side of the road, tossing white crests into the rapids that mirrored the snowy peaks in the distance.

Mount McKinley loomed large to his left as Ben spotted the sign for Tugat. He turned right and slowed the car to a crawl. A one-lane, metal-framed bridge with wooden slats crossed the river, it looked worn but sturdy.

Ben felt a little nervous crossing the bridge, but he saw no other choice. The car crept forward as the bridge creaked and moaned under its weight. Ben began to press the accelerator as he neared the other side. The brush to one side swayed and separated to allow a moose to step out of the bushes and onto the gravel road. He had no option but to stop. The bridge groaned in response.

Ben's eyes widened. The moose stopped and stared straight at him. It was the largest animal he had ever seen, easily ten feet tall at the top of its massive rack of antlers. Muscles rippled beneath its brown fur as it moved. The creature nearly spanned the width of the road. The bridge sighed again.

Ben glanced in the rear-view mirror and quickly decided that reversing back to the highway wasn't an option. When he looked forward again, the moose was still staring directly at him. Then, just as suddenly as it had appeared, the animal gave a slow nod and stepped into the brush on the far side of the road. It was as if a guard had allowed him to pass into a kingdom he had yet to reach.

Ben's heart pounded. He took a deep breath and drove onto solid land.

CHAPTER 3

BLUE SKY AND BEAR NECESSITIES

The drive from the bridge into town was no more than a mile. The majestic view faded beneath a canopy of spruce and paper birch. Eventually, the forest gave way to a small-town buzzing with activity. Ben drove into the center of the town, a place filled with architecture of mixed Eastern Orthodox and early log cabin. Ben couldn't see where there had been any plan in laying out the city with the exception that it had one main street. Harsh weather had left its marks on the town though there was a feeling of agelessness about it. Ben saw a large sign mounted on the side of a building that read "Blue Sky Saloon." He pulled into an empty spot between two pickup trucks in the unmarked area beside the saloon.

Two picnic tables seemed randomly placed in front of the saloon. Steps led up to the entrance and along the side of a sprawling front porch. Behind the building, a small fenced-in area barely concealed an open back door to a storage space and a large, padlocked waste bin. On the side where Ben parked, windows opened on the side of the building with curtains that fluttered in the breeze.

Ben got out of the car and stretched after the long drive. He glanced around what he guessed was "downtown." There were a few houses, a general store, a two-story office building, and a curious shop with iron yard art and large rocks scattered out front. The town couldn't have been more than four city blocks in total, and Ben had already seen most, though not all, of what it had to offer.

As he climbed the stairs, Ben passed a few people. Each one nodded or greeted him with a "good morning." On the far end of the front porch, a couple in their early twenties had their backpacks open and contents spread out in front of them. They hunched over, taking inventory and talking intently. The entrance to the saloon featured two large, heavy wooden doors propped open. Ben walked through and was met with a cool rush of air. He stepped into a cavernous room filled with people.

Some were nestled up to the bar along the back wall; others were at various stages of their meals at the many tables. A large moose head was mounted above the bar like a watchful sentry, silently inspecting everyone who entered. The walls were covered with photos of pioneers and climbers. Between the pictures, frontier memorabilia of all kinds filled the gaps, some of it so old, it looked like it hadn't been touched in decades.

Hunger and the smell of hot food reminded Ben it was time to eat. He walked over to the bar and asked the man sitting beside an empty stool, "Is this seat taken?"

The man half-turned and replied, "Not if you've decided to sit in it."

Ben sat down and watched as a white-haired woman moved swiftly back and forth, delivering steaming plates of food and refilling drinks. She danced through the chaos, a warm smile never leaving her face.

As she passed Ben, she dropped a menu in front of him without breaking stride.

He scanned it. Items like Bear Mash, Salmon Candy, and Sure Shot caught his eye. In the center, outlined in bold red, was the Denali Deluxe, a five-pound hamburger made from a blend of different meats, served with a full pound of fries. The menu claimed the challenge was to eat it all in 30 minutes or less. Ben enjoyed a challenge. Would that be one he could take?

Ben shook his head, uncertain. He turned to the man beside him, who appeared absorbed in a newspaper pulled from a stack on the bar. "Any suggestions on what's good?" Ben asked.

The man laid the paper on top of the pile and turned toward him. "Well, that depends on how hungry you are. I think the meatloaf's the special today."

All the strange names and ingredients from the menu flashed through Ben's mind. He asked, "What's in it?"

The man chuckled. "Ground beef, onion, ketchup, stuff like that. Haven't you ever had meatloaf before?"

Ben flushed slightly, then tried to shift the conversation. "So... you like reading the news, huh?"

The man placed his hand proudly on the stack of newspapers. Ben was surprised to see the Oregonian on top. "I like to stay informed. I subscribe to sixteen daily sources from around the world in four different languages. I never skip a page, or a puzzle."

"Wow," Ben replied, genuinely impressed. "I barely find time to read the local paper. Most of my news comes from NPR and the Techcrunch Podcast."

The man turned on his stool to fully face Ben. "That's part of the problem with people today. They gather information only from local or national sources designed to sway, not inform. Perspective matters, and it can't be hidden, if you're open to seeing it. #16: True character always reveals itself." He turned back to the counter and resumed reading.

Ben blinked, thinking about the man's words, then turned to face the counter himself.

At that moment, the whirlwind of a woman Ben could only describe as small, bubbly and smiling appeared from behind the bar, stepped up to him and asked, "What'll you have, darlin'?"

"I hear the meatloaf is the special. And an Arnold Palmer," Ben replied.

She disappeared as quickly as she'd arrived, and somehow, in her flurry, a tall glass of the swirling drink, no ice, appeared in front of him.

Ben watched the crowd while he waited for his meal. It was an odd mix: young adults dressed like models in a Patagonia commercial and older folks who moved more slowly. The latter had more of a local feel to them.

"Here you go, sweetie," the woman said, placing Ben's lunch in front of him. "If you need anything else, I'm Lizzy. Just let me know."

Ben opened his mouth to thank her, but she had already moved on to the next customer.

Ben took a bite of the meatloaf and paused to savor the flavor. He wondered if he could actually taste every ingredient. Chewing slowly, he tried to enjoy it as much as possible.

As he ate, a man walked up to him on the service side of the bar. "Well… what do you think?"

Ben swallowed and took in the question. The man looked out of place in the bar, his short, neatly kept brown hair and bright green eyes gave him a polished appearance. Dressed in a golf shirt and slacks, he could have passed for a New York attorney.

Ben replied, "It's delicious. My compliments to the cook."

"That would be me, and thanks," the man said with a smile. "I've got to tell you a secret: before I moved here, I'd never cooked a thing. Most of my meals came from restaurants, not my own kitchen."

Ben half-grinned. "Well, you've learned something."

The man shot back, "Let's not make that the case, okay? By the way, I'm Jason. This is my place. I hope you like it."

"Oh," Ben said with surprise, "I was supposed to find you when I got here. I'm Ben Reeves."

Jason smiled broadly. "Of course you are, I can see it now. You're Scott's boy. I'm sorry for your loss."

Ben paled as his heart dropped at the comment. He hadn't expected to be recognized so quickly. "Yeah… his attorney said you might be able to help me get to his house."

Jason's smile dimmed, though he made no move to speak right away. A few moments passed before he finally said, "Why don't you finish eating, and we'll take care of that. In the meantime, maybe Anthony can tell you about the weather in Istanbul or something."

Without waiting for a response, Jason turned and walked toward the kitchen.

Ben felt a bit lost and wasn't sure what to do next, so he turned back to the guys sitting beside him. He carefully folded the paper he was holding and glanced at Ben.

"So, you're Anthony, I guess?" Ben asked.

Anthony laid the folded paper on the stack and smoothed it with his hand. "That's me every day."

Trying to be quick-witted, Ben asked, "What's the weather like today in Istanbul?"

Anthony didn't smile. He looked at Ben seriously and replied, "Eighty-six and twenty percent chance of rain. But a gusher is coming along any day now."

Ben wasn't sure if he was being serious or not, so he changed the subject. "What's with all these kids around here? There are a bunch of them."

Anthony surveyed the bar like he was seeing it for the first time. Finally, he spoke. "This is the jumping-off spot for a lot of people heading into the park or climbing the mountain." He drew in a breath and seemed to be thinking. Then he continued as though he were lecturing a hall of students, "For the God-awful reason of honoring President William McKinley, a prospector started calling the mountain by the president's surname back in 1896. Officially, the name stuck until 2015, when it reverted to its actual name, Denali. In the native language, that means 'tall' or 'high.' Earlier this year, the feds decided to switch it back."

Anthony leaned closer to Ben and added, "I suggest you use her maiden name."

Ben tried not to laugh at the serious reproach. "Was this guy serious?" he wondered.

Anthony leaned back and shifted the stack of newspapers to get a better grip on them. Ben turned back to his plate and continued eating. Anthony stood for a second, watching Ben, before adding, "Your dad used her rightful name."

Ben gave Anthony a short wave in response and kept eating, while Anthony headed toward the door with the stack of newspapers.

Ben scraped the last of the meatloaf from his plate just as Lizzy reappeared.

"Well?" she asked with a nod toward the plate. Ben gave her the OK sign with his free hand.

"That'll be sixteen dollars," she said. "Let me know when you're ready to go."

Ben swallowed the last bite and raised his hand to signal her to wait. He pulled his wallet from his front pocket and counted out the cash onto the counter. "Thanks, Lizzy. That was delicious. I need to get to my father's house, can you tell me how to get there?"

Lizzy pulled a roll of bills from her apron and added his money to it. She looked at Ben for a long moment. She lifted her hand to her mouth and dropped her eyes in an effort not to cry. "You look like him. I'll tell Jason to come over and talk to you," she said.

Ben glanced away in an effort to not lose his own composure and turned the subject with a question he hoped felt lighter, "Why won't anyone just tell me where his house is? What's the big deal?"

He turned back to the crowd and waited. Several minutes passed before Jason returned.

Trying to stay polite, Ben asked, "Would you mind giving me directions to my dad's house?"

Jason leaned against the bar.

"Stand up," he said without malice, yet a commanding and practiced patience in his tone.

Ben was caught off guard by the sudden command, but he obeyed. Jason looked him over, then asked, "Do you have another pair of shoes, maybe even some boots?"

Confused, Ben answered slowly, "No. I only brought one change of clothes. No extra shoes."

Jason scoffed. "You're not going to make it to your dad's house in a pair of loafers. You need to talk to Hakkon."

Ben took a step back, still unsure. "What? Who?"

"He owns the general store across the street. You can't drive to your dad's house, and you definitely can't get there dressed like that. Tell him you need something more suited for the environment."

Ben felt a flicker of anger rise in his chest. He also felt like he was backed into a corner, with no real choice. He asked, "If I get something more suitable, will you help me already?"

Jason's tone softened. "Listen, this back country is no joke. Get suited up, and I'll take you there myself."

Ben gave a reluctant nod. He didn't like being ordered around, but he could kind of see Jason's point. He stepped out of the tavern and onto the dirt road that ran through the center of town. His destination was easy to spot: a weathered wooden sign hung above a squat building, its large blue letters reading Bear Necessities General Mercantile.

Ben looked up at the sun, still hanging high overhead. It hadn't seemed to move since he arrived.

Ben walked across the street and into the store. Large glass windows displayed a wide variety of goods at the front, but they were nothing compared to what lay inside. A single bare bulb hung from the ceiling, casting shadows over the mounds of merchandise that filled the room. The walls were lined with shelves and assorted sundries, while the center of the store held an enormous table piled with furs, artifacts, and other items Ben couldn't begin to identify. He wandered in awe down one of the aisles.

At the end of the table, a large open space appeared near the back of the store. Ben's eyes were drawn to shelves that stretched from floor to ceiling along three walls, packed with books. There had to be thousands of them. "Enough to fill a library, maybe," he thought.

Off to one side stood a small wooden counter topped with a vintage cash register that looked like it belonged in the nineteenth century. A thin man sat on a stool behind the counter, his hair so blond it was nearly white. His chiseled Nordic face was buried in the book he was reading. He didn't seem to notice Ben enter.

Ben coughed.

The man looked up in mild surprise and lowered his book to the counter. "What can I do for you?" he asked, his accent thick and heavy.

"Hasson?" Ben asked.

The shopkeeper smiled and his eyes twinkled. "I don't know who this Hasson is. MY name is Hakkon as in hawk on a high perch. Tell me who you are, and what I can do for you."

Something about Hakkon's demeanor made Ben feel welcome, almost at home. "I need some shoes. More accurately, I need something I can wear to hike."

Hakkon stood up and walked around the counter, stopping in front of Ben. He glanced down at Ben's feet. "Size eleven," he stated confidently. "What kind of hiking are you doing? Climbing?"

"No, nothing like that," Ben replied in a softer tone than he intended. "I just need to get to my dad's house." He immediately wondered why he'd shared that last part. This whirlwind trip had pulled emotions to the surface he hadn't been completely ready to deal with.

"I see," Hakkon said, rubbing his chin. "Your dad lives around here?"

"Yes, well. No," Ben said. "He passed recently, and…"

Hakkon watched him for a moment, then cut in. "You're Scott's son. He told me about you."

The words hit Ben like a punch to the chest. "He told you about me?"

"Are you still doing that... what's it called? Kiteboarding?" Hakkon asked enthusiastically.

Ben felt his cheeks flush. "Not in a long time. I play a lot of pool now."

Hakkon didn't seem to notice. He kept talking. "Number three. You can do anything, the hard part is narrowing it down. But you're not going to make that walk dressed like you're headed to a party. You'll need looser pants, a long-sleeve shirt... and some bug juice."

"Okay, I guess. I'm a size," Ben started.

"I know," Hakkon said, already walking toward another part of the store where clothes were neatly stacked. "Size 32 waist, 34 inseam, large shirt. Stand right there."

Hakkon moved through the store, shifting from one stack to the next, rummaging through bins. He slowly built a pile of clothes on the counter beside the register. Then came the energy bars, a water bottle, and a handful of small items.

Ben finally asked, "How far is his house? Looks like you're gearing me up for a backwoods adventure."

Hakkon smiled but didn't stop moving. Eventually, he finished packing. He folded the clothes neatly and loaded them into a light-framed backpack along with the other items.

Ben watched, then asked defensively, "What's this going to cost me?"

Hakkon smiled again. "Don't worry, I'll put it on your tab."

Ben felt tension in his shoulders increase. "I don't know if I want a tab. I won't be here for more than a day or so."

Hakkon nodded. "I understand. We can settle up when you leave. You'll have to come back through town to get your car anyway."

Ben sighed. He wondered if he was being treated like some kind of rookie tourist. He'd hiked extensively around Oregon. It wasn't like he was new to this kind of thing. Finally, he gave to resignation, which did make him feel a little better. Perhaps, it was better not to make waves. He admitted to himself that everyone did seem to be helping him with no apparent alternative motives.

CHAPTER 4

THE WALK TO THE CABIN

Once Hakkon had him fully geared up, Ben slung the backpack over his shoulders and made his way back to the tavern. He walked in and spotted Jason near the end of the bar. "Hey, I think I'm ready to go."

Jason looked at his watch and considered for a moment. "Let me get Tommy to cover the dinner rush, and we'll get you where you need to go."

Ben ducked into the men's room to change. He felt silly wearing a long-sleeve shirt on a sunny summer day, but Hakkon had insisted. He had said something about mosquitoes being big enough to carry off babies. When he returned to the bar, he waited. And waited. The crowd began to swell. More grizzled men filtered in. Ben felt his patience thinning just as Jason reappeared, a shorter, stockier version of him following close behind. Jason noted Ben's gaze on the other man and indicated with a nod and the explanation, "My brother, Tommy."

Tommy smiled broadly and acknowledged Ben with a quick wave of his hand.

"Let's go," Jason said without ceremony. He turned and headed for the door. Ben hesitated, then hurried to sling his backpack into place and catch up.

They reached the main street, and Jason turned north without stopping. Ben called out from several feet behind, "Hey, can't we drive at least part of the way?"

Jason stopped, turned toward Ben, and shook his head. "Not where we're going. Come on." Then he turned back and kept walking.

Their path ran parallel to the highway for a while. A rushing river separated them from the road. The brush was sparse but tall, the ground dry and sandy. In the west, Denali towered over the horizon, the sky painted in colors you'd expect to see only in a French painting. Ben found the walking easy as long as he paid attention to where he was stepping. Jason seemed to be following a path Ben couldn't see. In fact, Ben felt very disoriented. He checked the sun several times to get an idea of the direction they traveled. He couldn't tell. The sun hung motionless in the sky and cast long shadows on the brush as they plodded through it. He wondered if Jason had noticed it at all.

After about an hour, Ben found a large rock and plopped down onto it. Jason took notice and stood beside him, fishing a bottle of water from his pack.

"How much farther?" Ben asked.

Jason glanced toward the horizon, taking a silent measure. Then, without a word, he resumed walking in a northerly direction.

"Hey, wait up!" Ben called as he scrambled to catch up.

Another hour passed. The river curved east, and so did they. The ground turned to tall grass and stone as the loamy soil gave way. The terrain grew steeper, and soon Ben realized they were walking through a valley. He pulled his iPhone from his pocket, only to find he didn't have a signal. He had no idea what time it was. His legs ached. His back throbbed.

He desperately wanted to sit. Ben wanted to stop and rest, but Jason kept walking. He didn't look tired at all, and he didn't slow down either. The valley walls rose higher and higher until Ben couldn't see their tops. Now and then, he caught some movement on the peaks, but he couldn't tell what it was.

Finally, Ben had to stop. He bent over, gasping for breath, and called out to Jason while pointing to a ridge on the right.

"What's that moving up there?"

Jason looked annoyed by the delay, but he paused. He followed Ben's finger, squinted for a moment, then said, "That's a Dall sheep. Good eating, if you can catch one. Heck of a climb to get to them. Even harder to get them down, if you do."

Ben was still breathing hard, hands on his knees. "I don't know if I can go much further," he said.

Jason smirked. "You won't have to. We'll drop down over that ridge line, and the cabin's just over there."

Ben lingered, taking the chance to rest. "What's your story, anyway?" he asked. "You don't look like a mountain man."

Jason grinned to himself. "I'm not. Or maybe I wasn't. I came up here after I lost my job back East. Had no idea a place like this even existed. Lizzy bought us tickets to help me get over the shock of getting laid off, and we never went home. That was... eight, nine years ago? I don't really remember. That life feels like a distant dream now." Ben could tell that Jason carried no regrets from that far away place.

Ben began breathing more steadily. "That's amazing. I find it hard to believe anyone would just walk away from their life, their roots, their family."

Jason stared at Ben for a moment and replied, "It happens more than you might imagine. Let's go. I'll be lucky to get home before midnight."

Ben looked at the sun hanging lazily in the sky and followed him.

True to Jason's word, the valley came to an abrupt end. They stood at the top of a long ridge overlooking a wide valley blanketed in wisps of tall grass and scattered wildflowers in every color. Light danced across the surface of a stream that wound through the field. Ben had seen many beautiful things today, but nothing compared to what he saw now.

Far off in the distance, he spotted a wooden cabin surrounded by a short fence, with a small storage building set off to the side. He thought he heard Jason mutter under his breath, "Life is short. Run and play naked. Number one."

He took in the view and wondered if he had heard Jason correctly. Jason didn't wait. He headed straight for the cabin.

He was several yards ahead of Ben. By the time Ben arrived, Jason was already inside. Ben walked through the door and dropped his backpack to the floor. A sofa took up most of the wall to his right, and he sank onto it, grateful they had finally arrived.

He glanced around the cabin, taking in his new surroundings. The living room and kitchen shared the front half of the house in one large, open space. Along the back wall were three open doors, one led to a bathroom, the other two to bedrooms.

Jason stood near an icebox with a beer in each hand. He drank from one and tossed the other to Ben. Ben caught it midair and took a deep drink. The golden liquid scorched his dry throat, just the way he liked it.

Breaking the silence, Ben said, "I'm wasted tired. It feels like the middle of the night, and judging by the sun, it can't even be five o'clock yet."

Jason chuckled and glanced at his watch. "Close. It's eight-thirty p.m. In Alaska, the daylight stretches long in summer and short in winter."

Ben laughed at himself. "I always thought that was an old wives' tale. How do you ever get any sleep?"

"You use blackout curtains in the bedroom. You'll see." Jason drained the last of his beer, tipping the can back until it was empty. He walked to the garbage can, opened the lid, and carefully sealed it shut after tossing the can in.

"Oh, and here's some advice," he added. "Don't leave garbage or food unattended or in open containers."

Ben frowned, puzzled. "Because it attracts bugs?"

Jason walked toward the door and, without turning around, replied, "Bears." The door slammed behind him.

Ben stared at the can in his hand. "Bears? Come on. He's probably just trying to scare me. Right?"

He sat on the sofa and let the long day wash through his mind. He rested until he felt some of his energy from the long walk return, then got up to explore the small cabin. Hunger gnawed at him. He checked the cabinets and found canned food, a can opener, and a propane camping stove. Dinner was quick, washed down with a couple of lukewarm beers from the refrigerator.

After eating, the fatigue from his long day caught up with him. He moved to one of the bedrooms, adjusted the heavy curtains as Jason had suggested, closed the door, and lay down on the bed fully clothed. He was asleep within minutes.

CHAPTER 5

NOZOMI AND THE BEAR

en had no idea how long he'd been asleep. He woke to a noise coming from the living area. "Bear!" he thought.

He scrambled out of bed, squinting to adjust his eyes to the semi-darkness. There was nothing in the room with any heft that he could use as a weapon. On the dresser, he spotted a large, plastic gold hairbrush. He grabbed it and crept toward the door.

"If it's a bear, maybe I should wait until it leaves," he thought. He stood at the door and listened. The noise continued. "I'll wait," he decided. "It'll leave in a minute." But the noise came closer, to the bedroom door.

Ben, unsure of what to do, raised the brush above his head like a hammer. The door creaked open under pressure from the other side. Light spilled into the room. He braced himself.

A shadowy figure, outlined by sunlight, filled the doorway and said, "Who are you, and what are you doing here?"

Ben froze as the figure came into focus.

"I've got my pistol pointed straight at you," she said. "Start talking."

Ben slowly lowered the brush to his side. He stared. She wasn't tall, maybe five-four or five-five. Slight build. Long black hair. He couldn't make out the color of her eyes, but he recognized the unmistakable squint of an angry woman, and the revolver she held at waist level. Ben stammered, "Let's not get carried away. I think I'm in the wrong place."

"You bet you are," she replied evenly.

Ben took a breath, trying to collect himself. "I thought this was my dad's cabin. I had a guide… I guess he brought me to the wrong one."

She didn't move. "Who's your dad?" she asked.

Ben spoke slowly. "Scott Reese. He used to live around here."

The woman seemed to relax, just slightly. She asked, "Scott Reese? Who are you, and why are you here?"

Ben didn't realize he'd been holding his breath until he let it out. "He died recently. I'm his son, Ben. I'm here because he wanted me to spread his ashes around this area."

The woman stood in silence, considering what he said. She lowered the gun to her side but didn't put it away. Backing into the living area, she commanded, "Come out here so I can see you in the light." Ben did as he was told.

She studied him and said, "Tell me something personal about him, something most people wouldn't know."

Ben paused. He hadn't thought about the details of his dad's life in a long time. Finally, he offered, "He moved here from Portland, Oregon, after he and my mom divorced. His birthday's sometime in May. He loved peanut butter and banana sandwiches. He called them Elvis-wiches."

The woman turned and walked over to a stuffed chair near the door. She sat down. "Yeah, he used to call them that stupid name." She rested the pistol in her lap, still watching Ben closely.

Ben slowly crossed the room and sat on the sofa. "Who are you?"

"Nozomi."

"Are you," Ben hesitated, unsure how to frame the question. He blurted it out. "Were you his wife? Or girlfriend, or…?"

Nozomi let out a sharp laugh, quick and cutting like a crack of thunder. "Of course not. We had… a living arrangement. We helped each other. It's how we do it in the outback."

Ben could tell the wheels were turning in Nozomi's mind. She spoke again. "Let me see his ashes."

Ben reached toward his backpack to retrieve them, then paused. "Can you put away that firearm first?"

She shook her head, smiling slightly. He continued anyway, his palms sweating as he pulled out the small ceramic urn and extended it toward her. He nervously eyed the pistol. She leaned forward, took it with one hand, and pressed her other palm flat against the pistol in her lap to keep it from sliding. Sitting back, she studied the urn in silence, turning it slowly from side to side.

When she was finished, she placed it unceremoniously on the small coffee table between them.

"Where are you going to spread them?" she asked.

"He said in his will he wanted me to spread them along Moose Creek."

Nozomi leaned back and went quiet again. Then she said, "Nope."

Surprised by her blunt response, Ben tried to defend his father's wishes. "It was what he wanted."

Nozomi looked at Ben evenly, without anger or sarcasm. "He'll be spread at his favorite place in the world. You can come, if you want."

Ben was taken aback by her abruptness. "Look, I'm just here to do what I think is right. I know you've got a gun, but we need to talk about this."

Nozomi's face lit up with a flash of amusement. She raised the pistol in her hand and glanced at it. "This? Don't worry about it. If I were going to shoot you, you'd already be dead." She stood and holstered the gun in a sheath strapped to her leg.

"I'll tell you what," she continued. "We'll spread a little at Moose Creek, and the rest where it should be spread."

Again Ben didn't feel like he really had a choice, and she still had a weapon she could grab at any time. "Okay," he agreed.

He started to reach for the urn, but she bent forward and picked it up herself. "I'll hold onto it," she said flatly.

She moved toward the kitchen. "I'll cook us some breakfast. I need you to go to the tater hole and get some eggs."

Ben stood up. "I don't know what that is or where to look."

She turned, clearly exasperated. "You really are a greenhorn. Go around back. You'll see a metal barrel buried mostly in the ground. It's like a refrigerator.

We don't have electricity out here, so we dig down to the permafrost. Helps keep food fresh longer."

Ben headed for the door, but she called after him, "Thanks for finding my brush. I've been looking for it."

He blushed, realizing he'd still been holding it. Gently, he set it on the coffee table and stepped outside to retrieve the eggs.

Nozomi cooked a delicious breakfast on the small camp stove, including some meat Ben couldn't identify. She made coffee too, so dark and thick you could probably stand a spoon in it.

They sat at the small kitchen table and ate in silence.

When they finished, she said, "We'll leave in a few minutes. Take these dishes down to the stream and wash them. When you get back, I'll be ready to go."

Ben didn't argue. He gathered the dishes, grabbed a scrub brush from the kitchen window, and made his way to the stream. The water was ice-cold and crystal clear. He could see small, round pebbles covering the bottom. He had to wash a dish and take a break, because the water would turn his hands blue. He stacked the dishes and cups as he worked. When he finished, he scooped up the dishes and stood.

He hadn't heard a sound, yet just a few feet away stood a black bear, staring back at him. The bear rose up on its hind legs. It tilted its head back and forth in a motion that made Ben think it was sniffing the air.

Ben didn't move. The bear didn't advance or retreat. He tried to remember what he'd learned in Boy Scouts. Was he supposed to lie on the ground and cover his head? Raise his arms in the air? Run? No, he knew running wasn't the answer, and his legs felt like jelly. He couldn't have walked away even if he'd tried.

The dishes fell from his hands. The clatter startled the bear. It replied with a guttural bark and slack jaw that dripped with saliva. Ben could count its teeth. For a second, he wondered if he could smell its breath. No, it wasn't that close.

A sharp crack split the air behind him. Only the bear's eyes moved as it glanced around the area where Ben stood. Then it dropped to all fours and walked away, disappearing into the tall grass.

Ben slowly turned back toward the cabin. Nozomi stood with a pistol pointed at the sky. She shook her head and said, "Greenhorns," before walking back inside.

Ben gathered the dishes he had dropped and followed her in.

The two quickly gathered what they needed. Nozomi carried the urn in a small pack slung over her shoulder. She handed Ben a bright yellow rope, neatly coiled. He draped it around his neck so that it rested on one shoulder and fell diagonally across his chest.

They reached the creek again fairly quickly. Nozomi removed the urn and took out just enough remains to fill one palm. She looked at him and asked if he wanted to say any final words.

"That doesn't look like much," he replied with a pang of guilt he wasn't fulfilling his stated obligation to even be here.

She dropped the ashes into the water and said, "Small creek, small deposit," before turning and walking away.

Ben started to object but couldn't find a reason to keep arguing, so he ran to catch up with her. She was a force to be reckoned and he felt a longing to see how he fit into the world that made her so self-assured.

CHAPTER 6

FATHER'S FAVORITE PLACE

They didn't travel far. The canyon walls surrounding them were steep, towering above like giant stone slabs. At a point only she recognized, Nozomi stopped. Ben looked up but couldn't see the top.

She handed him a climbing harness. She clipped a bag of white chalk to her belt and attached several carabiners.

"I'll lead," she said, placing her hand on the rock wall and starting to climb.

Ben waited until she was about ten feet off the ground before beginning his ascent. He felt more at ease when he saw her run the rope tied between them through a chock she placed in a crack on the rock wall. He did his best to follow the path she took. Within seconds, he was fifty feet up. Ben paused on a small ledge and looked skyward, Nozomi was already well ahead, only stopping occasionally to check an anchor or place another chock in place.

He grabbed the next rock hold and pushed upward.

The climb didn't take long. Nozomi had already vanished over the top edge before Ben reached it. He liked the strain in his muscles as he reached for a crevice and planted his fingertips inside it. The breeze curled around him like a quiet encouragement. For a moment, he felt weightless, even free in a way he couldn't recall feeling before now. Sweat rolled from his hairline down his neck, and it was a sensation he didn't want to forget. He had climbed before. But this? This was next level.

Ben pulled himself over the ledge at the top. Nozomi was sitting cross-legged on a patch of dirt, going through the pack she had brought. She acknowledged Ben when he arrived. "Maybe you aren't such a tenderfoot. Come sit over here," she said, patting the ground beside her.

"Not dropping me off the wall back there is certainly encouraging," he said jokingly.

She playfully added, "There's still time." They both chuckled.

He removed the coiled rope and sat where she indicated. Ben looked at the scene before him. Rough ledges, close to the same height as where they were, dotted the near landscape. Behind them rose tall mountains, some disappearing into billowy white clouds. Above it all stretched a sky that shifted from light to deep blue the higher you looked.

"This is it? His favorite place?" Ben asked.

"No," Nozomi replied, pulling an urn from the pack and standing. "You'll see. Follow me."

She began walking along the widening ledge, dotted with bare shrubs and the occasional wildflower. The path sloped upward gently and led them through a small thicket. Ben stepped through and stopped suddenly beside Nozomi.

They stood at the edge of a crystal-clear pool. Its sides and bottom were made of black lava stone. The pool was forty or fifty feet across, and the sky reflected on its surface so clearly that you could see the clouds move and shift shape. They took in the view.

"This mountain is an extinct volcano, as many are in this area," Nozomi said. "Sometimes, if you're lucky, you'll find pools like this one, collecting rainwater and melted snow."

Ben could see why this was his father's favorite place. It looked as if God had pressed a thumb against the earth and left this perfect imprint.

Nozomi set the urn on the ground, stripped down to her underwear, and dove into the pool. The sky scene broke into ripples, then quickly reassembled, each piece of the picture snapping back into place. Ben felt a tug at his heart and wiped a tear from his cheek.

"Why are you waiting?" Nozomi asked as she treaded water.

Ben pulled his shirt over his head, stepped out of his socks and boots, dropped his khaki field pants to the ground, and dove into the clear water.

He broke the surface with a yell. "OH SWEET JESUS, this water is cold!"

Nozomi laughed and floated on her back, swimming across the pool. Ben ducked beneath the surface, holding his breath as long as he could. He moved from end to end, side to side, unable to remember the last time he'd felt so invigorated.

The two swam and splashed each other until they were completely exhausted. Nozomi proved to be an excellent swimmer as everything else Ben had witnessed her do. They climbed onto the shore and dried themselves as best they could with their hands. Sitting on the edge of the pool, they sat quietly.

Ben broke the silence, "Does this place have a name?"

Nozomi replied, "The natives say, when you know a place and you know its stories, then you know what that place is for."

"I don't get it."

"It means that what makes a place special goes beyond just a name. A name can be superficial. There's a deeper context, knowing the history, or what a place gives to the people who live in it, that matters more than simply labeling it."

Ben tucked this new information away. He'd have to think about it, though he understood how this unnamed pond made him feel connected to the world in a different way. He agreed, there wasn't a single word that captured that feeling.

They poured Scott's dust into the water and watched it drift across the surface, then dissolve and sink into the pool. Nothing was said. No final words, no hollow effigies. Scott was now part of the earth he had loved.

They got dressed again and walked back to the edge of the cliff they had climbed. Nozomi uncoiled the rope while Ben fastened his climbing harness. She doubled the rope, hammered anchors into the rock, and set the rappel line.

Ben looked over the edge and braced himself for the trip down.

Nozomi tested the ropes and said, almost absentmindedly, "Number ten. It's not about the danger. It's about the safety."

"What did you say?" Ben asked. Frustration welled as he recalled other points during this trip.

Nozomi clipped into the line and started walking backward toward the edge. "What do you mean?"

"The whole time I've been here, people keep saying these numbers and then things that make absolutely no sense to me. You said something about danger and safety."

Nozomi stood poised to rappel. She considered what Ben said and replied,

"Your dad had all these sayings. He told them all the time, and after a while, if you spent enough time with him, you found yourself saying them too. One of them was number fourteen: 'Being immortal is easy. Leave good memories with the people around you. They will tell your story.'" She stepped back and dropped out of sight.

Ben felt alive in a way he couldn't remember. They walked back to the cabin.

"I think about him sometimes," Ben said casually.

Nozomi didn't look at him. "He talked about you all the time," she said. "He really loved you."

Regret seeped into Ben's heart. "He never called. Never sent a card."

Nozomi looked down at her feet as she considered her reply. "You're a grown man, Ben. It's just as far from here to Oregon as it is from Oregon to here. He was trying to respect your wishes."

A small flash of anger surged through Ben's veins. He tried to keep his voice steady, but it cracked. "I was the kid. He was the dad."

Nozomi didn't break stride, though she glanced at Ben, who caught her gaze. "Things aren't always that simple, Ben. He was trying not to hurt you, just like you were trying not to hurt him. Adults make bad decisions sometimes."

Ben smiled slightly. "You're pretty wise, aren't you?"

She returned the smile. "A lot of it came from your dad."

She picked up the pace, and Ben jogged to keep up.

Back at the cabin, they prepared dinner together. Nozomi built a fire in front of the cabin, and they sat by it, watched the flames. Ben told her about his childhood. They had moved there when he was very young from Tennessee. He reflected how full his life had been and now he realized he had not appreciated it as much as he might have. She shared her life as an Army brat. The bases, the schools, the friends had changed frequently, but she had seen things as a child she realized many would never see. One of her stories related an art teacher in Michigan talking about art in the Louve. When she told the class she had been there on a field trip, the teacher didn't believe her and called her mother about the "wild" stories she told. She laughed at the memory of her mom correcting the teacher.

Ben didn't want it to end, but he knew he needed the rest. He would head back to town tomorrow, and Nozomi would guide him. A coyote howled in the distance. "They don't usually get this far north," Nozomi remarked. "Must've found a good hunting ground."

Ben nodded, even though he wasn't sure. He just wanted this connection he felt to Alaska, to Nozomi to last.

Nozomi doused the fire with spring water while Ben headed to bed. That night, he slept in his father's room. He noted the sound of Nozomi's bedroom door closing. He slipped beneath the quilt, wondering as he drifted off if it might have once belonged to his grandmother.

The next day, Nozomi was cooking breakfast when Ben rose from bed. He sat up and stretched, then looked around the room for clues about who his father had become. His father had left behind few possessions. Ben figured there hadn't been much need for luxuries out in the bush.

Something on the dresser across the room caught Ben's eye. He got out of bed and padded over to it. Sitting on top was a small gold frame holding a faded photo of himself in his Cub Scout uniform. Behind him stood Scott, his hand resting on Ben's shoulder. Ben was holding an arrow and a certificate, symbols of his graduation from Cubs to Boy Scouts. Both of them were smiling, clearly proud. Ben remembered that night, the sense of accomplishment, the pride, the connection to his dad, who had helped him earn that achievement. A tear slid down his cheek, and he wiped it away.

He looked around the room, momentarily lost in thought. Finally, he picked up the photo and slid it into his backpack. Slinging the bag over his shoulder, he went out to eat breakfast with Nozomi.

CHAPTER 7

FAREWELL TO TUGAT

en felt melancholy on the walk back to town. Nozomi kept pace with him, saying little. Ben breathed the clean air deep into his lungs and tried to commit every detail of the journey to memory.

Ben stepped through the brush. The town took a new hue in his mind's eye. The tavern was just as busy as the day he had left. Nothing had changed in the little town, though something had changed in Ben. He couldn't say exactly what it was, only that something inside him felt different.

Ben and Nozomi sat at the bar. Lizzy appeared faster than an online rumor.

"Hi, Lizzy," Ben greeted her cheerfully.

"Hey, sweetie. What can I get you?" she asked.

Ben looked at Nozomi.

She asked, "Should we toast to your sendoff, tenderfoot?"

Ben nodded gently and looked into her brown eyes. He thought he might have seen a tiny gold fleck twinkle in one of them.

She ordered, "Make it two Duck Farts, Lizzy."

Lizzy poured the layered drinks as they waited. Ben laughed. "There's so much here I still have to learn."

Lizzy raised her glass with them and toasted, "Miners come and go. The gold runs hot, and the gold runs cold. Without the help of the horses and dogs in the snow so deep, we'll find the miners in the thaw, for in the cold, their bodies will keep. To the horses!"

A few old-timers around the room shouted, "Hear, hear!" and "Salute!" The three downed their drinks in a single swallow.

"Thank you, Lizzy," Ben said.

He turned on the stool toward Nozomi, tracing her face in his mind, etching every detail into memory. "Thank you," was all he could manage.

She smiled gently. "You can always come back," she told him. "We know you here now, and there's one thing your dad used to say that kept us all together."

"One thing?" Ben asked.

"Well, one of many. He said, 'You're family, or you're not.' You have a home here, when you want it."

Ben nodded. He stood and walked toward the door. "Yes," he thought. "I'll be back."

THINGS MY DAD SAYS

17) Living a good life is simple. Make the next right decision. If you wouldn't do it in front of your dad, it isn't the right decision.

16) True character always reveals itself.

15) Everyone pays their dues, now or later. Go ahead and get it out of the way.

14) Being immortal is easy. Leave good memories with the people around you. They will tell your story.

13) Respect is once given, twice earned.

12) Someone is looking to you as a role model right now. Don't short change them.

11) Try it twice to make sure you don't like it.

10) It's not about the danger. It's about the safety.

9) If you wouldn't do it to a total stranger, don't do it to your family.

8) Only moderation in excess.

7) Church is for sinners. Don't be afraid to associate with your own kind.

6) Having a drink is fine. Making an ass out of yourself isn't.

5) Friends are there for the good AND the bad.

4) You haven't failed until you have given up.

3) You can do anything. The hard part is narrowing it down.

2) You're family or you're not.

1) Life is short. Run and play naked.

ABOUT THE AUTHOR

SCOTT PARISH has enjoyed a long and varied writing career. He previously hosted the regional television cooking show, *Guys Cook Too,* and the *Dying to Eat* podcast, which he wrote much of the scripting. His passion for storytelling extended to print, where he served as a food columnist for *Hey Y'all* and *Good Ol' Boys* magazines.

Scott is the author of several self-published books, including *Tiger at the Table*, which explores table manners, and *Shiloh Just Right*, centered on themes of self-esteem. His fictional works include *Biloxi: A Story of Hope* and *Swamp Jesus*. He also collaborated with Arcadia Publishing on *Images of Madison County*, documenting the history of his Tennessee hometown.

Now he resides in Florida, where life is simple, slow and unencumbered. Just the way he likes it.

If you want to reach Scott, write him at readscottsbooks@gmail.com